FRIENDS
OF ACPL

Nymphaea alba

Rubus fruticosus

Lysandra coridon

...hoides non-scripta

Nicrophorus vespillo

Succisa pratensis

Coenonympha pamphilus

Strangalia maculata

Sedum anglicum

Mnium hornum

Hamearis lucina

Inachis io

Bellis perennis

Adalia bipunctata

Hyles lineata

Rosa canina

Sorbus aucuparia

Centaurea cyanus

Stellaria media

Vicia cracca

Fritillaria meleagris

Cirsium vulgare

Filipendula vulgaris

Colostygia pectinataria

Leucojum aestivum

For Amy, amazing and
wonderful editor
and friend

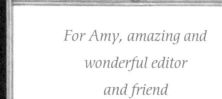

Dryopteris filix-mas

For my mother

All
for the
Newborn
Baby

Anagallis arvensis

Phyllis Root

illustrated by
Nicola Bayley

CANDLEWICK PRESS
CAMBRIDGE, MASSACHUSETTS

The inn was full.

It was cold in the stable,

dark and bare.

But Mary held her baby close,

and when he fussed,

as babies do,

she sang a little cradle song

all for the newborn baby.

$\mathcal{H}$ush now, baby,

In the manger,

Donkey shares

His sweetest hay.

Oxen breathing

Warm beside you,

Keep the winter

Cold away.

Woolly sheep

Kneel all around you,

Make a fleecy

Place to rest.

Wren weaves moss

And leaves and feathers,

Softly lines

Your manger nest.

Fireflies

Like tiny candles

Light the stable

Where you sleep.

Little fishes

In the river

Flash and splash

And laugh and leap.

Roses in the snow

Are blooming.

Sun and moon

Shine in the sky.

Nightingale

Up in the rafters

Sings his sweetest

Lullaby.

Cherry tree

With branches bending

Offers cherries

Ripe and red.

Spider spins

A silken blanket,

Lays it on your

Manger bed.

*R*ooster cannot wait

Till morning,

Crows the news

About your birth.

*H*erons fill the sky

With flying,

Crying *joy*

To all the earth.

Hush now, baby,

In the manger.

All the world

So bright and new

Waits for you, my newborn baby.

Hush and sleep

The whole night through.

Sleep,

my newborn

baby.

Fragaria vesca

First edition 2000

Library of Congress Cataloging-in-Publication Data
Root, Phyllis.
All for the newborn baby / Phyllis Root ; illustrated
by Nicola Bayley. — 1st ed.
p. cm
Summary: Mary sings a lullaby to the newborn baby Jesus as
He lies in the manger, and in her song she describes how the
world around Him is rejoicing at His birth.

ISBN 0-7636-0093-8

1. Jesus Christ — Nativity — Songs and music — Texts.
2. Lullabies, American — Texts. [1. Jesus Christ — Nativity —
Songs and music. 2. Lullabies.] I. Bayley, Nicola, ill. II. Title
PZ8.3.R667A1 2000
782.4215'82'0973—dc21—98-17231

Printed in Hong Kong

This book was typeset in Cerigo Book.
Calligraphic initials by Robin Brockway.
The illustrations were done in watercolor.

Candlewick Press
2067 Massachusetts Avenue
Cambridge, Massachusetts 02140

Ornithopus perpusillus

Tagetes patula

AUTHOR'S NOTE

When I was a child, I read that on
Christmas Eve at midnight the stable animals
speak, and if you are blessed you might
hear them. The image of the animals
talking together stayed with me.
I began to search in old carols and stories
and found more Christmas miracle tales —
donkeys and sheep from many countries, but
especially Italy, oxen from France, a wren from
Belgium, fireflies from England, fish from Puerto
Rico, roses from Germany, a nightingale
from Catalonia in Spain, a cherry tree from
Appalachia, a spider from Poland, a rooster
from Mexico, and herons from Spain.
Slowly these began to weave themselves into
a cradle song that Mary might have sung —
all for the newborn baby.

Papilio machaon

Gentiana verna

Trifolium campostre

Trifolium arvense

Campanula rotundifolia

Crataegus monogyna

Ligustrum vulgare

Viola tricolor

Agrotis exclamationis

Lampyris noctiluca

Humulus lupulus

Phalaena venosa

Chrysopa septempunctata

Zygaena filipendulae

Pieris brassicae

Cardamine pratensis

Hedera helix

Capsella bursa-pastoris

Eupithecia centaureata

Muscari neglectum

Wahlenbergia hederacea

Nymphalis polychloros

Plantago lanceolata

Rumex acetosella